Tennis and Toes

Beth Phillips

To order additional copies of this book, contact:
Xlibris
844-714-8691
www.Xlibris.com
Orders@Xlibris.com

ISBN: Softcover   978-1-6698-2977-5
         EBook   978-1-6698-2976-8

Print information available on the last page

Rev. date: 06/14/2022

This book belongs to:

~~~~~~~~~~~~~~~~~~~~~~~~~~~~~

Grateful Acknowledgements to Northdale
Golf and Tennis club, Carrollwood country
Club. USTA and Ultimate tennis leagues.

For me tennis is part about the game, reading your opponent and the lifetime friendships. Stick with the winners is what I was told. Personally, I have learned many things about terms like sportsmanship, humility, resolving conflict, integrity, focus, strategy, securing your match with tennis balls and these are the many folks that I learned from. Often times off court topics come to light as well. I was able to apply a similar strategy subbing in the schools when a tornado watch was issued.

2001. Lantana shared many off court stories with me about her childhood and the Cold War drills spent in basements with lights out. She taught me not to play when one has an injury. I was able to apply a similar strategy when subbing in a local school system when a tornado watch was issued. Not the same scale but never the less similar.

Xenon taught us what to keep in a tennis bag. In other words to be prepared. He bought two new tennis racquets every 7 years. He changed his serve at an older age. He taught us sportsmanship by always shaking your opponents hand at the end of a match. He taught us to be a good sport. Also shared stories of Cold War drills as well. Getting under desks at school. I was able to use being properly prepared with the summer rains in Florida.

Onyx taught me things not to say or do. Making comments about my people's attire. Flo taught me to be alert at the net. Sometimes conflict needs to be resolved regarding line calls and everyone handles it differently. Some will walk off the court and others will offer to play the point over. I was able to use for my own use during Hurricane Irma by buying supplies that were needed.

Amber taught me about believing in yourself. Purple who was once teacher of the year taught me about consistency. We played every Thanksgiving until her mother passed and she had to stop playing on Thanksgiving because she had to help prepare the food. Purple also taught me about consistency and winning. One time I was up 5-2 and lost 7-5 because of not running up to get the continued drop shot. I was able to use this skill in a later match.

Black reminded me to give myself permission to quit thinking. JB...Some people are either able or not willing to follow rules. For example, spinning to see who wins the choice of serve at the start of the game and have to be reminded.

Orange used to try to hit me with the tennis ball to see if I was paying attention.

Plantation reminded me to secure oneself making sure someone knows CPR when playing in the heat. Beige taught me accountability by one time I was late and she said I should run laps. Playing her once, she said she sees it as practice.

Crimson reminded me the importance of reading your opponent and no excuses! Seeing weaknesses in your opponent. Also not always staying in your own home court. Grey taught me that some people's weakness could be waiting for lob shots. Most people have some form of a weakness whether it covering the court or waiting for lob shots.

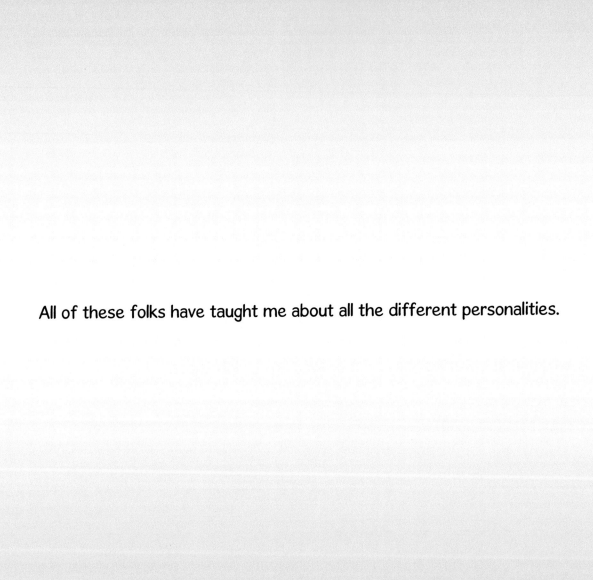

All of these folks have taught me about all the different personalities.

Printed in the United States
by Baker & Taylor Publisher Services